On this date

_____

a **Fairy Godmother**

appeared in the Wonder Window to help

_____

(Name)

discover the beauty, love and spirit in

every living creature.

Illustrated by Martha-Elizabeth Ferguson.

ISBN: 0-9634910-8-3

Library of Congress Card Number: 2001088275

10 9 8 7 6 5 4 3 2 1 First Edition March 2002

Printed in China

My Fairy Godmother

Samara Anjelae

In memory of

Daisy and Bigfoot

A special thanks to Isabella, a literary cat.

BelleTress Books

While we each have a Guardian Angel, a Fairy Godmother is a gift given only to those who appreciate and respect nature and all living creatures – from the tiniest of insects to the largest of animals. Your Fairy Godmother can be a Lady of the Woods, a Guardian of the Sea or a Garden Spirit. To be enchanted with a Fairy Godmother, we must find a secret gateway to Fairyland. It is then, and only then, that we can hope to have a visit from our Fairy Godmother.

The Fairy Gateway lies in every Wonder
Window. If you believe in fairies, you will
find fairies. Look closely and you will see
them. Fairies are the little people who
carry the life force that gives nature its
color, form and beauty. They are
busy helping make the grass
greener, the trees stronger, and
the flowers more beautiful.
Fairies will bring you ideas,
make you smile and laugh,
and show you the secrets
of nature.

Fairies are very talented. They can change their size and appearance at will. Their shapes are often free flowing and hard to describe. These bright beings can have wings like angels or they can look like humans. They can be tiny or of considerable size. It depends on the particular work they have to do. Fairies usually dress in the clothes and follow the customs of the land in which they live.

Those who can see fairies are individuals who are at peace with nature – Mother Nature lovers. People who work with their hands – artists. Souls who are wise – seers. Beings who are kind and giving – humanitarians. And Fairy Helpers – those who are kind to animals.

A Fairy Godmother has Special Powers

Playing Music

Foretelling Events

Making you Sleepy

Bringing Good Luck

Drawing Animals Near

Delivering your Wishes

Appearing and Disappearing

Keeping Secrets and Treasures

Working Magic with the Weather

Before you enter
Fairyland, you must learn
the fairy rules. Do not talk about
fairies in a bad manner or they will leave you and
you may never see them again. Say thank you when a fairy leaves
you a gift such as a feather along your path, a special stone, the beautiful
scent of a flower or a lost item returned. Do not tell anyone about the
presence of a fairy without first asking permission from your fairy friend,
and if it is supposed to be a secret, then keep it a secret.

When you see mushrooms in a circle, be respectful and step around
them. It is a fairy ring. When you spot trees with a hollow hole filled with
branches and twigs, know that it might be a fairy or animal home and
should be left alone. Learn by watching fairies and animals in their natural
habitat, not by capturing them.

Fairy Signs

Sparkles of light around plants and flowers

Items vanishing and appearing again

Sudden unexplained goose bumps

Unidentified music and singing

Bending of grass blades

Sweet scents of flowers

Uncontrolled laughter

Puzzling loss of time

Soft crinkling noises

Rippling of water

Delicate breezes

Fairy rings

FAIRY GODMOTHER ALPHABET

F is for Finding Fairies when no one else does.

A is for Appreciating Animals and the Little People.

I is for Inviting fairies into your life.

R is for Receiving nature's gifts.

Y is for Yielding to fairy requests.

G is for Giving to Mother Nature.

O is for Opening your heart to fairy love.

D is for Deciding to believe in fairies.

M is for Making Magic with the Wee Folk.

O is for Offering your help to animals.

T is for Thinking about the wonders of the world.

H is for Hearing with your Heart rather than with your ears.

E is for Entering Wonder Windows.

R is for Resting assured that you have a

Fairy Godmother

Fairies love to celebrate. On
Fairy Festival Days they come from
the water, air and earth to dance,
sing and enjoy Mother Nature. Fairy
Festival Days include the Autumn and
Spring Equinox. This is when the sun
crosses the equator and day and night are
equal. They also celebrate the Summer and
Winter Solstice when the sun is farthest from
the equator. The equinoxes and solstices mark
the beginning of each season. Other reasons
for celebration include a Shooting Star,
a Morning Moon, a Rising Red
Sun, a Radiant Rainbow and
Your Birthday.

Are you drawn to the water, or would you rather be near a campfire? Do you like to watch the birds in the air, or be out in a garden working with the soil? There are many types of fairies. Turn the page to discover the earth, fire, air and water fairies.

Earth Fairies are also known as gnomes. They like to work with stones and minerals and create jewels. Gnomes live in trees, bushes, grasses and plants. They frequently have long beards, wear red caps on their heads, and dress in materials which they create. They pay little attention to humans because they are busy working and caring for their own families. The best times to see and talk to the earth fairies are when they are resting.

Fire Fairies are known
as salamanders, not to be confused with
the animal known as the salamander. Behind
every fire there is a Fire Fairy that helps make the
flame. They are small, usually between two to twelve
inches. Fire must be controlled and respected if it is
to be of benefit to fairies and to the environment.
They will work hard to build a fire if your
intention is wise, like a campfire where
storytellers bring laughter and
closeness. Fire Fairies like it when
you ask for their help and thank
them for their kindness.

Air Fairies are known
as sylphs. They plant creative ideas in
your mind. These divine beings can be
colorful in their dress, or if they choose,
they can become invisible. Many times a
fairy comes up with an invention and
passes it on to an earth being. When you
are creating art, or just feeling inspired to
create something, pay attention and see
if you have an air fairy helping you.

Water Fairies are
known as undines or water spirits.
You can see them riding the waves of
the ocean, dancing on lakes, resting on
marshy land, or fluttering around
flowers that grow in watery places.
Undines are clothed in a shimmery
substance that resembles floating
chiffon. They usually have wings of gold
and silver. The best time to spot water
fairies is at sunset and sunrise.

Fairy Likes

Daisies

Animals

Rainfall

Gardens

Laughter

Ladybugs

Butterflies

Honeybees

Dragonflies

Lilac Bushes

Storytelling

Kind People

Secret Places

Magic Wands

Sparkly items

Animal lovers

Hidden treasures

Children (little people like themselves)

Fairy Dislikes

Trouble

Loud Bells

Dirty Water

Unclean Air

Forest Fires

Grumpy People

Startling Noises

Harmful Chemicals

Unflattering Fairy Tales

Anyone who disrespects Nature

Messy rooms (except for closets)

Fairies are drawn to beautiful stones
Learn about sacred gemstones such as
sparkling emeralds, rubies and sapphires. Be
a detective and decipher fairy symbols. An
acorn means love, a four-leaf clover means
good fortune and hearts mean devotion.
And then there are those mysterious
symbols that only you and your Fairy
Godmother will share together.

Make a Fairy Godmother Treasure Chest.
A decorative box or a pretty container will work.
Include notes about your wishes, hopes and
special treasures. Try writing a story or poem
celebrating the beauty of nature. Be outside in the
presence of fairies when you compose your piece. Each
time you add to your chest, know that your Fairy
Godmother will keep your treasures safe and secure.
When you make an effort to express your love for the
earth, you are helping to build a better place for all.
Remember, every tree, rock, flower and animal
has something to teach us.

Fairy Colors

Really Red

Bonkers Blue

Go-Go Green

Purple Passion

Yappy Yellow

Boomerang Black

Glittering Gold

Laughing Lavender

Chilly Chartreuse

Fun Fuschia

Oops Orange

Artful Aubergine

Wild White

Silly Silver

Fairy Delight (rarely seen)

To the eyes, stars do not
look like they have much color. Yet, like
fairies, they actually range in hue from red to
purplish white. Remember stars are only
visible at certain times, just like your Fairy
Godmother. Search the Fairy Kingdom,
especially around flowers, and you will
find the gateway to Fairyland.

Fairy scholars recommend the "tween times" and "tween places" for spotting fairies. The "tween times" are those times that are undefinable. Dawn and Dusk – neither day or night. Noon – neither morning or afternoon. Midnight – neither one day or the next. "Tween places" are places in the natural world that are neither one place or another. It is the intersection of two worlds, like lakeshores, where glades grow in the woods, or at fences and border hedges. Extend an invitation to meet the Wee Folk at a "tween time and place."

Fairies are called by many different names. Sometimes they want their names to reflect their true identites. Through history, some tales portray fairies as mischief makers. Some of them are, but for the most part, they have only good in their hearts. To find fairies, learn how to address them by their favorite names.

Devas

Gentry

Wee Folk

Little People

Moss People

Tree Shadows

Bright Beings

Nature Spirits

Forgetful Folk

People of Peace

Good Neighbors

Elves

Trolls

Pixies

Sprites

Gnomes

Brownies

Elementals

Leprechauns

Keepers of Memories

Sidhe (people of the hills)

Mother Nature's Children

Be Like a Fairy

Sing Often

Be Colorful

Ride a Horse

Talk to a Tree

Notice Beauty

Rest by Water

Paint a Picture

Listen to Birds

Be a Storyteller

Help an Animal

Be around Flowers

Play an Instrument

Shimmer in the Sun

Take a Nature Walk

Find a Kitten Purring

Make a Dog's Tail Wag

Walk Barefoot in the Grass

And when others say they don't believe in fairies, or in a Fairy Godmother, smile and go on. One day when they live in harmony with nature, they will discover Wonder Windows, where fairies exist and dreams come true.

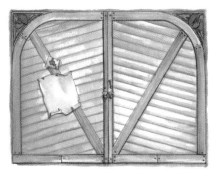

Wonder Window Series

A collection of timeless books that are a treasury of soul wisdom,
making them fine gifts for all ages.

Other books in the Wonder Window Series:

My Guardian Angel, an enchanting
book that promotes a deeper understanding
of angels and our relationship with our
Guardian Angel. A Guardian Angel is
assigned to every soul's Wonder Window for
guidance, love and protection throughout
the journey of life.

My Magical Mermaid, a mesmerizing
book that journeys into the mysteries of the
seas. A Magical Mermaid arrives in the
Wonder Window sharing the gifts of the sea,
the treasures on earth and the magic in life.

BelleTress Books

On this date

_____

(Birthday)

a **Guardian Angel**

was assigned to the Wonder Window of

_____

(Name)

*for guidance, love, and protection
throughout the journey of life.*

Illustrated by Martha-Elizabeth Ferguson.

ISBN: 0-9634910-7-5

Library of Congress Card Number: 2001088274

10 9 8 7 6 5 4 3 2 1 First Edition March 2002

Printed in China

To Matthew and Jessie

BelleTress Books

Ask an angel to come into your life. The moment you ask is the moment your angel arrives. Guardian Angels are assigned at birth to every soul born. They come from the realm of heaven, where a pure source of love exists for all. When you open a window to your heart, even for an instant, you will find your Guardian Angel.

The word angel comes from the Greek word angelos, meaning messenger. Angels are thought of as messengers between God and humanity. The spirit of sharing, caring and communicating is part of the divine plan, a pattern of oneness among all created things.

Give your Guardian Angel a name or your angel may have already given the name to you. The name could come when you are singing, playing, or just being very still. Call the name when you are in the mood to talk to your special friend or when you want some love and guidance from your angel.

Make an angel a lifelong friend, messenger and companion.

Since the dawn of time, angels have graced us with their presence. Many cultures throughout the world believe in angels. Angels can come to us as:

Glowing beings
Pink balls of sparks
Helping spirits
Beams of light
Tingles on the neck
Sweet, unexplained smells
Intuition (a knowing)

Everybody experiences angels in their own special ways. These messengers bridge heaven and earth. They remind us of truth, beauty and goodness.

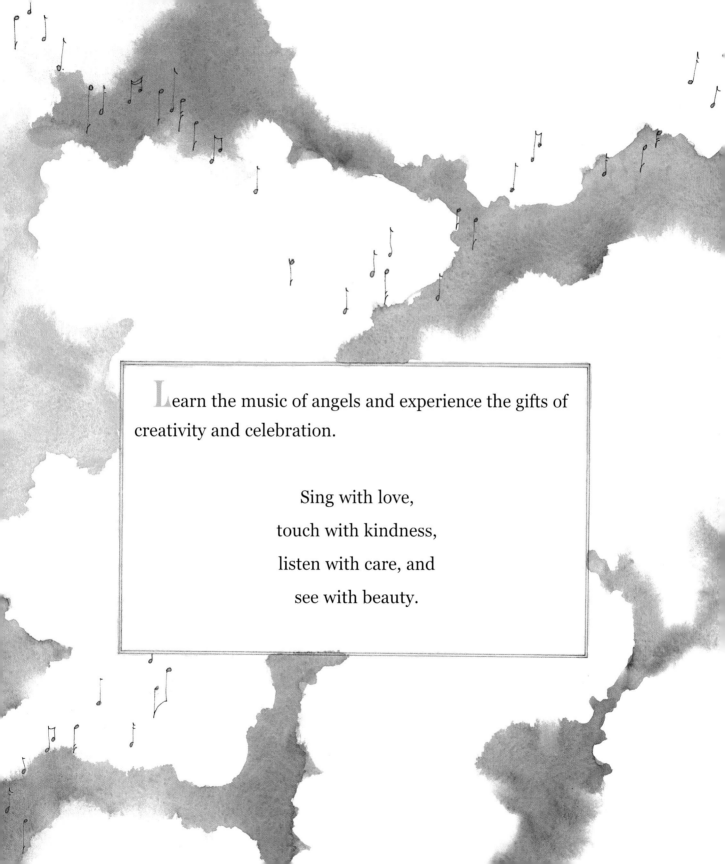

Learn the music of angels and experience the gifts of creativity and celebration.

Sing with love,

touch with kindness,

listen with care, and

see with beauty.

Special Sayings for the Week

Monday	Angel, Angel, come fly with me.
Tuesday	Help me make my day cheery and free.
Wednesday	Angel, Angel, bring me the best.
Thursday	Show me the way with all my tasks.
Friday	Angel, Angel, come create with me.
Saturday	Let's play throughout the day.
Sunday	Angel, Angel, let's say thanks and take a rest.

Take an imaginary walk. You may be in the woods, by the ocean, on a mountain, or at your home. Let your angel greet you as you wander. Next, imagine your heavenly friend handing you a gift. This gift or talent is one you already have but may have forgotten. Thank your angel for bringing you this idea that will help you become the best you can be. We are never given a hope or wish without also being given the opportunities to make it come true. As you grow, your gifts may change. Be aware of what your talents and dreams are today. There are no limits to creativity when angels inspire us. We just have to develop the ability to listen to our angels of inspiration.

GUARDIAN ANGEL ALPHABET

G is for Guidance that your angels bring.

U is for Understanding their soft messages.

A is for Always knowing that you are loved.

R is for Receiving angel blessings.

D is for Donating your toys or time to help others.

I is for Inspiring others to do the same.

A is for Appreciating the wonders of heaven.

N is for Noble acts that angels do.

A is for Accepting that everyone has a Guardian Angel.

N is for Never forgetting that angels are in your life.

G is for Giving your attention to kind thoughts.

E is for Enjoying your family and friends.

L is for Loving yourself,

Loving others and

Loving your

GUARDIAN ANGEL

If you need some love or want to love others more, call upon the Angel of Love. The Angel of Love teaches us to have deep and tender feelings of affection for others and for ourselves. Nurture the love in your heart, and share the love with others.

When you are feeling especially lonely and want some company, call upon the Angel of Friendship. The Angel of Friendship is ready to be a true friend – supportive, kind, considerate and respectful.

If you are having trouble being a good friend to others, ask the Angel of Friendship for guidance. This friendly angel is a never-ending source of goodwill, and is always available to help you spread your wings of kindness and acceptance.

Have you ever felt misunderstood or felt you were treated unfairly? The Angel of Fairness will help you honor your feelings, see a problem clearly, keep you honest and understand the actions of others. In time, the truth will be heard. All will come right and all will be well.

When you want to have fun, call upon the Angel of Play. This festive angel will make you smile, laugh and shine with light. Be ready to dance, skip, sing, and be filled with wonder. The Angel of Play brings good fortune, and is always inventing new ways to spread joy and happiness.

Celebrate Angels Every Month

January Tell the first person you see every morning that you love them. Start by saying an angel hello, "*halo*."

February Make snow or sand angels, and on a heartfelt day make your angel a valentine.

March Find a four-leaf angelic clover and make a happy wish.

April Write a poem about angels. Sing it to your angelic friends as they smile with delight.

May Joyfully take some crayons or paints and draw a picture of your Guardian Angel. Watch your angel come alive.

June Give your angel a treat. Make it nice and sweet. A big smile. An open heart. A happy halo. A kind word. A positive thought. A make-believe hug and a bite of your ice cream!

July	Be extra kind to all living creatures. Adopt, love, or care for a nearby animal. Try to see the world through the eyes of your animal friend.
August	On your back lie in the grass and find angels in the clouds.
September	Try to find the meaning of your name. The word angel means messenger. Know that you too are a messenger. Spread happiness this month.
October	Make something with your hands. While you create ask your angels to put their hands over yours.
November	Say a Prayer of Thanks. Enjoy your many blessings.
December	Leave out angel treats – plants, flowers, fragrances, beautiful cloths, peaceful music and best of all, your love.

When you are trying to figure out the difference between right and wrong, ask yourself, "What would an angel do in my same place?" When you have an answer, then carry on as an angel would.

In your heart you have hopes, wishes and concerns. When you pray you are sharing these thoughts. There are many ways to pray. Prayers are personal. You can pray alone or with others. You can pray to give thanks, ask for answers or ask for help. You can pray by singing, dancing, chanting, thinking, or even writing a poem.

God is my protector,
God is my light,
God is with me
Every day and night.
In this moment, I have all that I need.

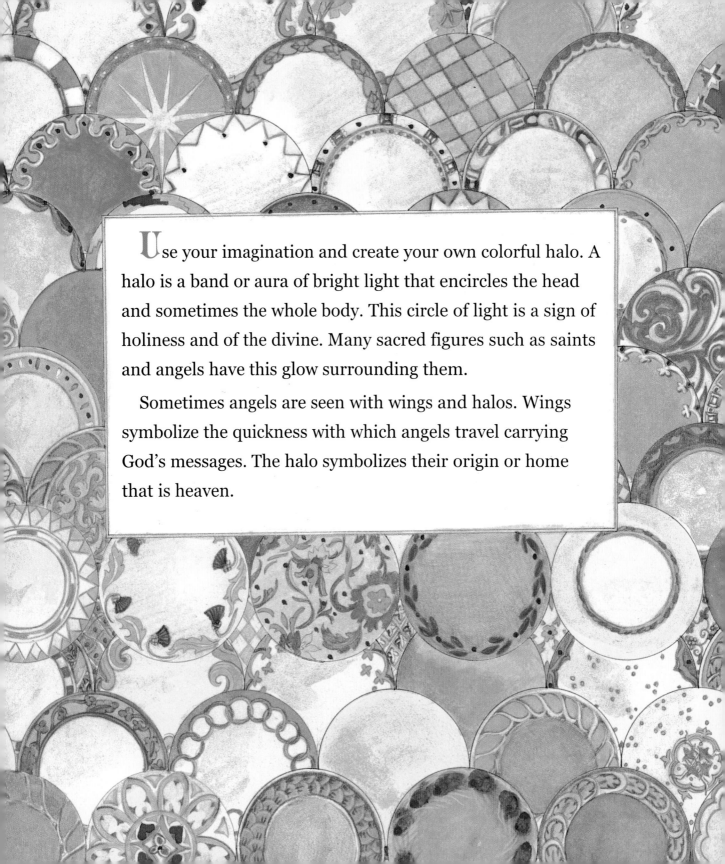

Use your imagination and create your own colorful halo. A halo is a band or aura of bright light that encircles the head and sometimes the whole body. This circle of light is a sign of holiness and of the divine. Many sacred figures such as saints and angels have this glow surrounding them.

Sometimes angels are seen with wings and halos. Wings symbolize the quickness with which angels travel carrying God's messages. The halo symbolizes their origin or home that is heaven.

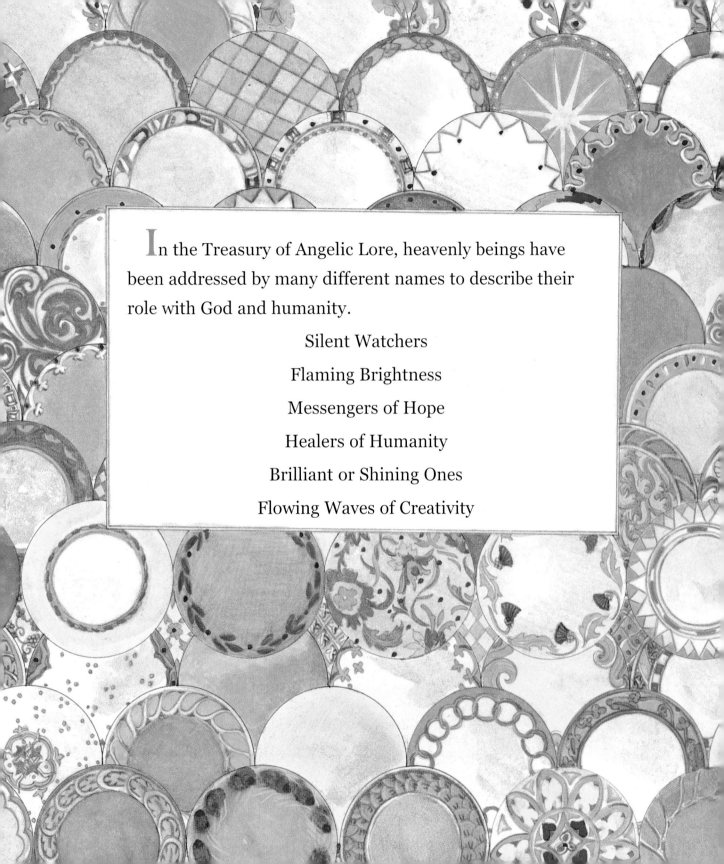

In the Treasury of Angelic Lore, heavenly beings have been addressed by many different names to describe their role with God and humanity.

Silent Watchers

Flaming Brightness

Messengers of Hope

Healers of Humanity

Brilliant or Shining Ones

Flowing Waves of Creativity

When you are feeling sick or unhappy, call on the Angel Heart Doctor. Imagine the angel is making a house call and is repairing your heart to make you feel better. Let the Angel Heart Doctor give you a dose of cheery medicine, such as:

Don't give up.

We like you just as you are.

Everything is going to be okay.

Soon your pain will be gone and you will be filled with warmth, love and light.

Be an Angel on Earth

- Leave flowers on someone's doorstep.

- Do something before you are asked.

- Smile at everybody. Let them wonder why.

- Hug an adult. You know they could use one.

- Whisper in someone's ear and remind them an angel is over their shoulder.

  - Write love notes and leave them for others to discover.

- Take a teddy bear, give it lots of hugs, and then give it to a person who might need a friend.

- Make a halo out of flowers and give it to someone who is especially nice.

Angels are approached
in only one way –

Love

The more you love yourself and the more you love others, the more you will be in the company of angels.

When the lights are out and you are having a hard time falling asleep, start counting angels. See how many you can count. Imagine what each angel is wearing, what color and shape they are, how they move, and what they have to say.

Tell yourself before you go to bed that you are going to remember your dreams. Angels bring us special messages in our sleep. In the morning, lie quietly for a moment and try to recall the detail of your dream. Then share your dream with a parent or a special friend. Know that all dreams, even the scary ones, are good. At night, we can work out our fears so our days are filled with joy. Dreams are part of God's plan, and some dreams are gateways to divine ideas sent by your Guardian Angel.

Sleep well.

Guardian Angel Reminders

Have Fun

Play Music

Say a Prayer

Make a Friend

Wear your Halo

Believe in Yourself

Spread your Wings

Give Something Away

Cry when you Need To

Always remember you have a Guardian Angel to guide, love and protect you throughout life. Open your Wonder Window to the world of wonder and awe.

Wonder Window Series

A collection of timeless books that are a treasury of soul wisdom,
making them fine gifts for all ages.

Other books in the Wonder Window Series:

My Fairy Godmother, an entertaining and
imaginative book that takes you into the realm of
fairies. A Fairy Godmother appears in the
Wonder Window to help you discover the
beauty, love and spirit in every living creature.

My Magical Mermaid, a mesmerizing
book that journeys into the mysteries of the seas.
A Magical Mermaid arrives in the Wonder
Window sharing the gifts of the sea, the
treasures on earth and the magic in life.

 BelleTress Books

On this date

_____

a **Magical Mermaid**

arrived in the Wonder Window to help

_____

(Name)

find the gifts of the sea, the treasures on earth,

and the magic of life.

Illustrated by Martha-Elizabeth Ferguson.

ISBN: 0-9634910-9-1

Library of Congress Card Number: 2001088276

10 9 8 7 6 5 4 3 2 1 First Edition March 2002

Printed in China

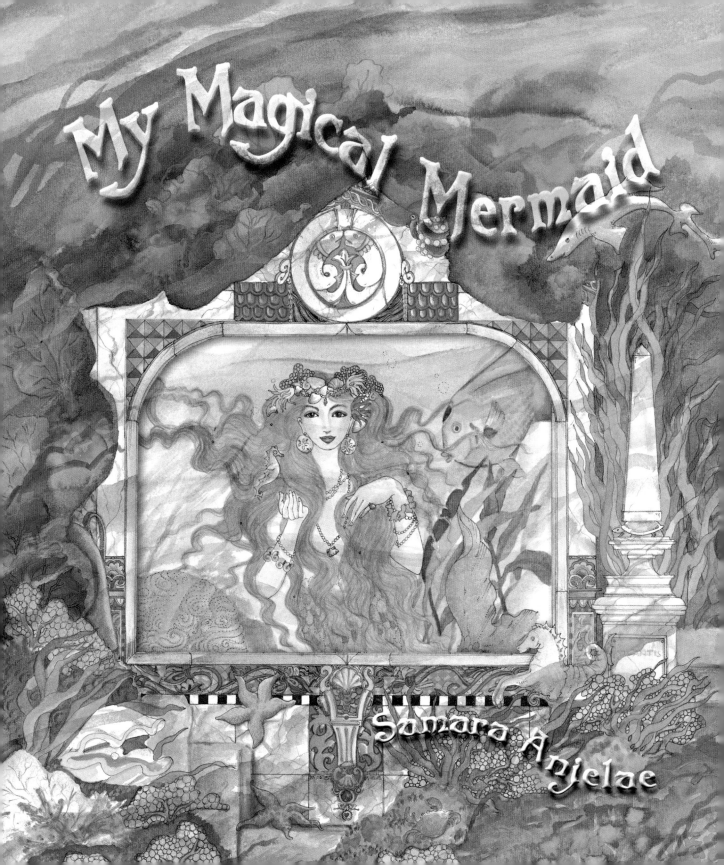

BelleTress Books

From the earliest Greek tales to present day accounts, mermaids have appeared in literature, art, and in sightings by fishermen and sea people all over the world. Mermaids are the mysterious ocean goddesses and gods that protect the sea and the sea animals. They live in and beneath the waters. Mermaids are known for having the ability to change their shimmery tails into human legs when they desire to walk upon dry land. No matter how long they stay on land, they are always said to be drawn back to the sea.

Mermaids warn birds of approaching storms, untangle octopuses, corral sea horses, and free playful sea pups caught in kelp beds. They are also known for their voices–a wonderful sweetness that can distract the best of seafarers. Mermaids sometimes annoy fishermen by removing the bait from the hooks to keep their fish friends from harm. Yet, in stormy weather they help fishermen arrive home safely. These ocean creatures make frequent trips ashore, if only to sit on a rock and comb out their long hair.

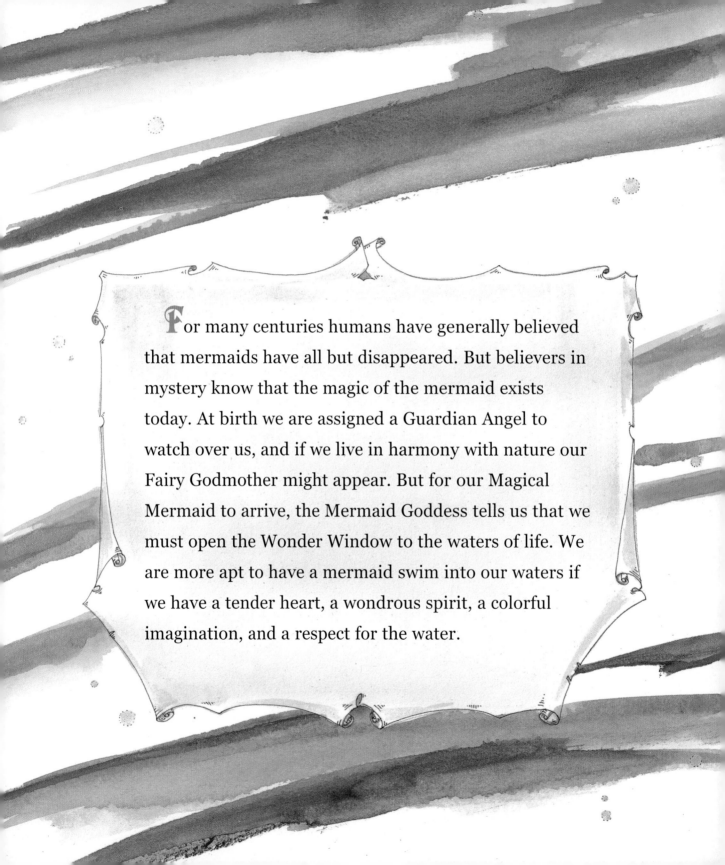

For many centuries humans have generally believed that mermaids have all but disappeared. But believers in mystery know that the magic of the mermaid exists today. At birth we are assigned a Guardian Angel to watch over us, and if we live in harmony with nature our Fairy Godmother might appear. But for our Magical Mermaid to arrive, the Mermaid Goddess tells us that we must open the Wonder Window to the waters of life. We are more apt to have a mermaid swim into our waters if we have a tender heart, a wondrous spirit, a colorful imagination, and a respect for the water.

While mermaids are faithful to the sea, they also have the desire to aid humans. Mermaids have many unusual powers. They can remind us that we are a part of nature and link us to the ocean of love. Mermaids can foretell events. They are able to predict storms at sea and trouble on land. They can also inspire humans to shine with color and create magic in their lives. Use your imagination to meet your Magical Mermaid. Imagine everything you can about your mermaid, then swim down through the waters to this magical realm.

The water covering seventy percent of the earth has always mesmerized humans. Without water there would be no life on land. Scientists and oceanographers have accomplished much in their study of marine life, yet they have not reached the depths of the sea. Mermaids live throughout the oceans in many colors, shapes and sizes. These Water Dancers live at the bottom of the seas in their many palaces and villages. In the Treasury of Mermaid Lore it is said that mermaids have love in their hearts, healing in their hands, talent in their tails and magic in their thoughts.

Dolphins are known as messengers between the mermaid world and the human world. If you spot one dancing and playing in the ocean, then know a mermaid might be near. Dolphins love to play, help and heal humans. Dolphins may visit mermaid villages, but they always emerge from their underwater travel to breathe and share their experiences. They inspire humans to be in a playful state, where our mood is light and our happiness shows. You can imitate the dolphin and discover the flow of breath by riding the waves of laughter and spreading joyful play and creativity.

The Magical Mermaid Alphabet

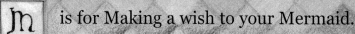

M is for Making a wish to your Mermaid.

A is for Admiring the beauty of the seas.

G is for Greeting your mermaid with a Grin.

I is for Igniting your Imagination with creativity.

C is for Caring for the water and the water babies.

A is for Anticipating your magical encounter.

L is for Living with splashes of color and fun.

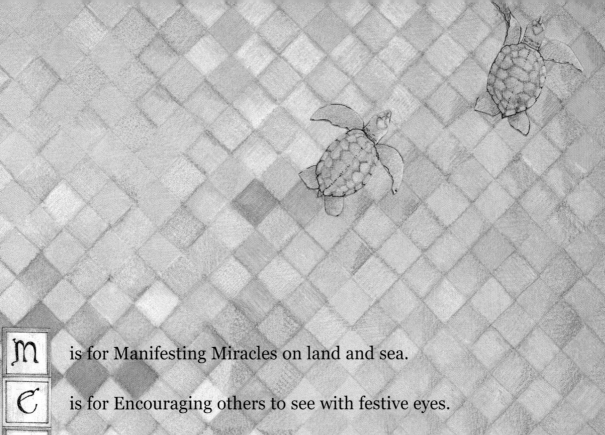

M is for Manifesting Miracles on land and sea.

E is for Encouraging others to see with festive eyes.

R is for Remembering the impossible is possible.

M is for Moonbathing with your shimmery friend.

A is for Awakening the land under the waves.

I is for Including others in your delightful discovery.

D is for Dancing through life with your

Magical Mermaid!

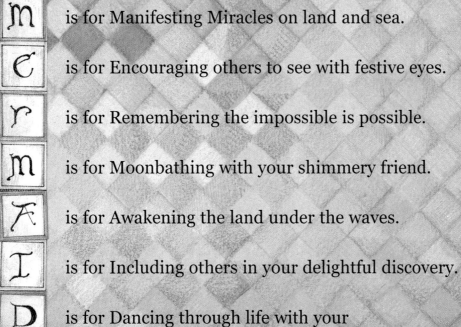

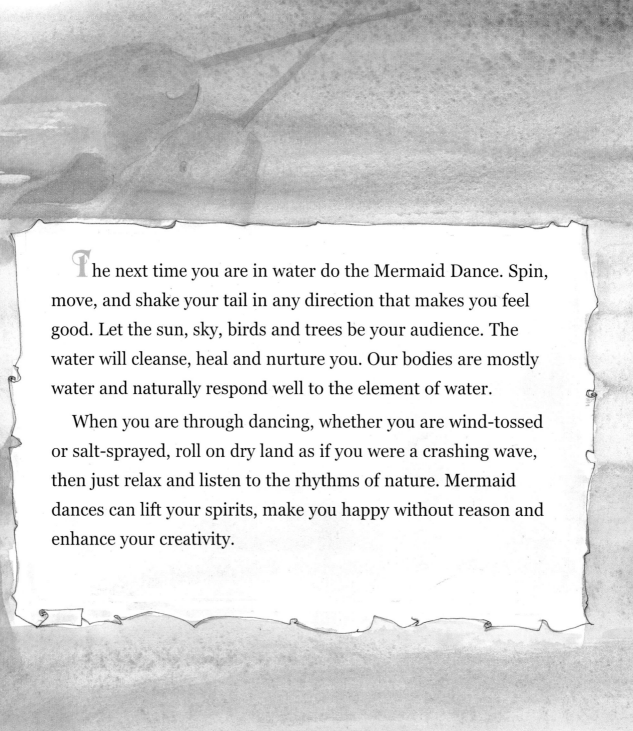

The next time you are in water do the Mermaid Dance. Spin, move, and shake your tail in any direction that makes you feel good. Let the sun, sky, birds and trees be your audience. The water will cleanse, heal and nurture you. Our bodies are mostly water and naturally respond well to the element of water.

When you are through dancing, whether you are wind-tossed or salt-sprayed, roll on dry land as if you were a crashing wave, then just relax and listen to the rhythms of nature. Mermaid dances can lift your spirits, make you happy without reason and enhance your creativity.

Have you traveled to other parts of the world? Our oceans bring the world together with the many shorelines that join different cultures and communities. Turn the page and explore the world map. Let the mermaids of the four great oceans take you on a journey.

The *Indian Sea Queen* is the guardian of the water from southern Asia to Antarctica and from eastern Africa to southwest Australia. The *Pacific Sea Queen* rules the largest of the world's oceans, extending from the western Americas to eastern Asia and Australia. The *Arctic Sea Queen* lives in the waters surrounding the North Pole. The *Atlantic Sea Queen* travels between the Arctic in the north to the Antarctic in the south between the eastern Americas and western Europe and Asia.

CHINA

JAPAN

PACIFIC OCEAN

EAST CHINA SEA

INDIA

BAY OF BENGAL

SOUTH CHINA SEAS

PHILIPPINES

SPICE ISLANDS

INDONESIA

INDIAN OCEAN

AUSTRALIA

AFRICA

MADAGASCAR

THE INDIAN AND PACIFIC SEA QUEENS

ARCTIC OCEAN

GREENLAND

ARCTIC AND THE ATLANTIC SEA QUEEN'

EUROPE

NORTH AMERICA

CARIBBEAN SEA

AFRICA

ATLANTIC OCEAN

SOUTH AMERICA

Friends of Mermaids

Traditionally, mermaids are regarded as a good omen.
These magical creature have a kinship with all life.

Sun

Moon

Stars

Fairies

Angels

Dolphins

Fish

Whales

Humans

Seals

Manatees

Starfish

Sea Horses

Sea Turtles

Sand Dollars

The sea people have languages all of their own – the true languages of love – that are never spoken.

The *Beautiful Language* is expressed by singing, chanting, and playing musical instruments such as cymbals, drums, flutes, harps and rain sticks.

The *Blissful Language* consists of kisses, blowing kisses, butterfly kisses, waves by hand or mermaid tails, hugs, grins, ear wiggles, handshakes, winks and double winks.

The *Heart Language* involves emotions and feelings. Just by thinking of something it can come true. Visualize what you want your Magical Mermaid to help you do. Keep your thoughts positive and pure and discover there is no language barrier.

Sea Guardians have been known to communicate with humans by using the *Beautiful Language*, the *Blissful Language*, and the *Heart Language* all at the same time.

Mermaids are inspired by the sound of peaceful music. On moonlit nights when most humans are asleep they join the land fairies and the angels to sing, dance and play. Mermaids link the rhythm of music to the rhythm of water. If you are fortunate, you can hear the enchanted tones of the Angelic Choir, the Fairy Carolers and the Mermaid Vocalists. They sing and play the Song of Oneness and rejoice to the blessings of life. They invite animals, children and kind people to join them in their celebration, either through their dreams or with their imaginative minds.

The Moon Lady is mysterious and beautiful. She changes her appearance a little every day and has many phases to her personality. Each time she changes her moonbeam, sparkles shed down on earth. When there is a Full Moon, mermaids make their presence known by leaving many magical gifts, sometimes called being "moonstruck." When there is a Half-Moon, mermaids give respect to those who feel different from others. They know how it is to be unusual since they can be half-human and half-fish at the same time.

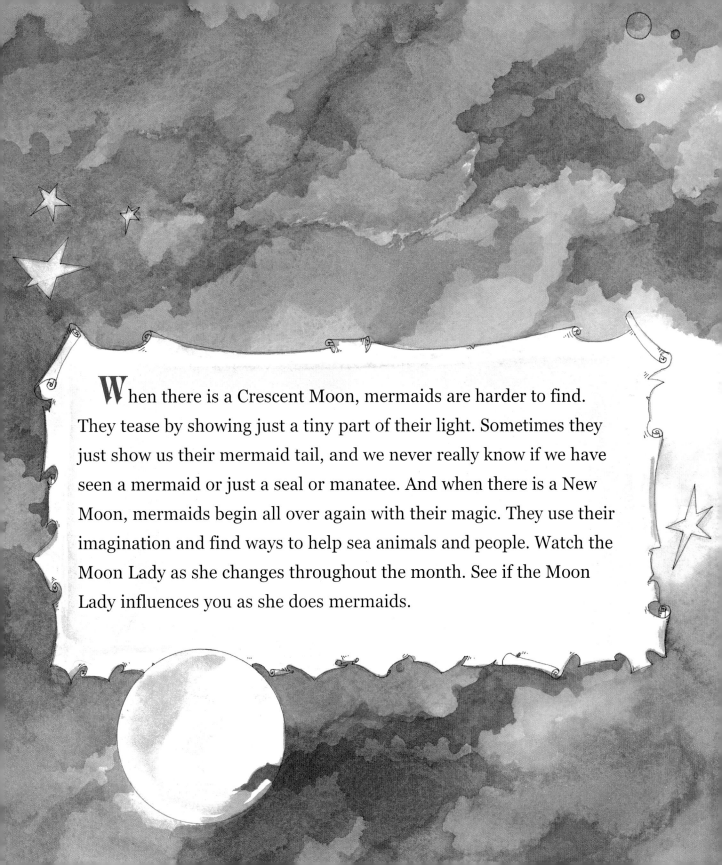

When there is a Crescent Moon, mermaids are harder to find. They tease by showing just a tiny part of their light. Sometimes they just show us their mermaid tail, and we never really know if we have seen a mermaid or just a seal or manatee. And when there is a New Moon, mermaids begin all over again with their magic. They use their imagination and find ways to help sea animals and people. Watch the Moon Lady as she changes throughout the month. See if the Moon Lady influences you as she does mermaids.

Wishing Well Wishes

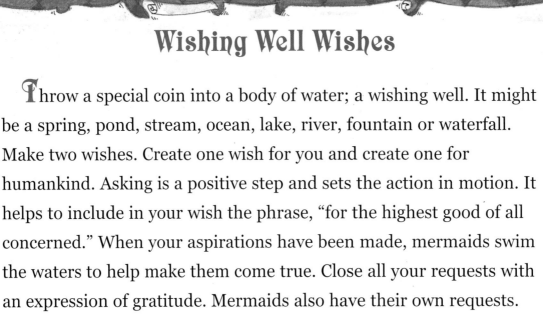

Throw a special coin into a body of water; a wishing well. It might be a spring, pond, stream, ocean, lake, river, fountain or waterfall. Make two wishes. Create one wish for you and create one for humankind. Asking is a positive step and sets the action in motion. It helps to include in your wish the phrase, "for the highest good of all concerned." When your aspirations have been made, mermaids swim the waters to help make them come true. Close all your requests with an expression of gratitude. Mermaids also have their own requests. Their global wish is that humans will make wise choices about their environment to ensure safe, clean and resourceful waters for today and for future generations.

Mermaid Wishes for You

Wild Hair

Moon Sparkles

Graceful Moves

Scales of Beauty

Splashes of Color

Stars of Compassion

Sweet Singing Voice

Shells of Splendor

Sea of Confidence

Mermaid Wisdom

Dolphin Intuition

Turtle Patience

Sun Smiles

Mermaids have been the subject of curiosity throughout time and have inspired works of music, literature and art. They have been called:

Water Dancers

Sea-Folk

Sky Watchers

Ocean Singers

Water Babies

Merpersons

Sea Guardians

Moon Bathers

Water Watchtowers

Sea Nymphs

Be Like a Mermaid

Watch the Sky

Play in the Sun

Frolic in the Water

Swim with Dolphins

Dance under the Moon

Splash in Rain Puddles

Take Swimming Lessons

Feed Fish and Marine Life

Comb your Hair in the Sun

Whistle in the Shower or Tub

Sing Love Songs to our Creator

Find Rainbow Light in Waterfalls

Shed a Salt Tear When you Need To

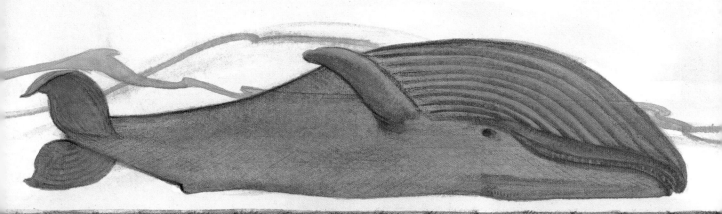

Remember, in every Wonder Window there are sparkling treasures. Keep on believing in yourself, in mermaids, and in the magic of life.

Wonder Window Series

A collection of timeless books that are a treasury of soul wisdom,
making them fine gifts for all ages.

Other books in the Wonder Window Series:

My Guardian Angel, an enchanting book that promotes a deeper understanding of angels and our relationship with our Guardian Angel.

A Guardian Angel is assigned to every soul's Wonder Window for guidance, love and protection throughout the journey of life.

My Fairy Godmother, an entertaining and imaginative book that takes you into the realm of fairies. A Fairy Godmother appears in the Wonder Window to help you discover the beauty, love and spirit in every living creature.

BelleTress Books